Dedicated to you. May you smile

The Storied Mind: A Descent Into Madness
Based on a true story
Written by: B. Humphrey

Copyright © 2024 by B. Humphrey All rights reserved.

No part of this book may be reproduced or transmitted in any form or by any means without the prior written permission of the author, except for the use of brief quotations in a book review.

All characters, movies, songs, and fictional scenarios belong to their original creators and trademark owners respectfully.

This is a work of fiction. Names, characters, places, and incidents are the product of the author's imagination or used fictitiously. Any resemblance to actual persons, living or dead, or actual events is purely coincidental.

Contents

Chapter One: A Cabin in the Snow
Chapter Two: The Echoes of Isolation
Chapter Three: First Signs of Dread
Chapter Four: Shadows in the Corners
Chapter Five: The Descent into Madness
Chapter Six: The Madness Deepens
Chapter Seven: Shadows and Hauntings
Chapter Eight: The Pull of Madness
Chapter Nine: The Descent into Isolation
Chapter Ten: Guilty Echoes
Chapter Eleven: The Breaking Point
Chapter Twelve: A Revelation

Chapter One: A Cabin in the Snow

Damien Crowe stood in the silence, his breath steaming into the frigid mountain air. Snow lay thick and unbroken around him, smoothing the landscape into soft, rounded shapes that swallowed sound, as if the world itself held its breath. His cabin sat nestled against a line of pine trees, small and weather-beaten, a lonely haven buried in the depths of winter. This, he thought, was what he wanted—a place where the only sounds were the whisper of snow on pine and the soft crunch of his boots breaking the surface. A place where he could escape.

But now, standing in its shadow, he felt the cold creep through his layers and into his bones, as if even the cabin resented being disturbed.

He exhaled, watching his breath rise and vanish into the still air, then turned to unload his bags. When he unlocked the cabin door and stepped inside, the silence deepened. He could almost hear it pressing against him as he stood in the doorway. Dust floated in narrow beams of light spilling from a single, small window. The air was heavy with the faint, musty scent of untouched wood and the stale loneliness of a place left to its own devices for too long.

The cabin was bare but serviceable, a squat room with walls the color of faded honey and a stone fireplace that took up most of one wall. A small kitchen nook sat to the right, with a low counter and an old stove whose paint had begun to peel, as if it, too, was wearing thin. Beyond the kitchen, a door led to a bedroom and a tiny bathroom—places he would explore later. For now, Damien simply stood there, taking in the quiet, trying to ease his pulse back into a steady rhythm. He'd wanted silence, but this stillness felt...watchful. As if the cabin itself had paused to consider his presence.

With a sense of ritual, he set down his bags, moving methodically, letting the familiar motions settle his nerves. As he unpacked, he caught himself murmuring aloud,

"He sets down his bag on the floor, straightens, looks around the room..."

He stopped, chuckling at himself. Too many hours spent narrating scenes had left a habit of bringing the voice into his own life. It was a reflex now, this detached observation of his own actions, as though he were both protagonist and author in some quiet drama. Silly, he thought. But the momentary laughter faded as quickly as it came, leaving him alone in the silence.

He released his cat, Sativa, from her carrier. She bolted out, a sleek shadow against the cabin's muted colors, her dark fur gleaming in the light. Within moments, she was darting from one end of the room to the other, batting at dust motes, pouncing on creaks in the floor, and pausing to arch her back as if something had startled her. Damien watched her antics, feeling a flicker of warmth pierce his lingering sense of isolation. Sativa was his constant companion—a creature of her own mind, independent and wild, as untamed as the mountains that surrounded them.

Watching her, he allowed himself to relax, sinking into the simple pleasure of her play. Sativa, with her stubborn defiance of domestication, always managed to remind him that there was life beyond the pages he wrote. When she'd finally finished exploring, she gave him a single, unimpressed glance, then began to clean herself, each movement precise, a ritual of self-care in an otherwise neglected space.

He turned to the small table by the window, setting up his laptop and notebooks. He liked to think of it as his "control center"—a place where he could reign in the stories clamoring to be written. He arranged everything with care: laptop centered, notebooks stacked to the left, pens lined up with a neatness that almost felt superstitious. Each item he set down seemed to absorb the quiet of the cabin, each sound vanishing into the stillness. It was a silence that both soothed and unnerved, as if the walls themselves were holding their breath, waiting to see what he would do.

Damien glanced out the window. Snow blanketed the ground, piling up against the trees, and beyond them, a vast mountain range spread across the horizon, jagged and ancient. The landscape was a monochrome of white and shadow, all color leached from the world, leaving only stark contrasts. Beautiful. Alien. A place stripped of everything unnecessary, leaving only the essentials—and, he hoped, a mind that could finally be quiet enough to think.

As he stood there, observing the silence and feeling its strange weight, he let his thoughts drift back to his past. This retreat into his mind is a familiar one; he's been building stories in his head since he was a child. Even then, he'd always felt a step out of sync with the world around him. Crowds made him feel claustrophobic, and school halls had always felt foreign, as if everyone else moved with a purpose he could never quite grasp.

While other kids had played together, he'd found his place in books and movies, drawn to characters who felt as disconnected as he did. His mother had understood. She, too, had a love for stories—she'd even written a few herself, though they remained unpublished, quiet dreams folded into the pages of notebooks left on the shelf. Some of Damien's earliest memories were of the two of them curled up on the couch, watching old movies, getting lost in worlds far more vivid than anything the real world seemed to offer.

It was there, in the stories they shared, that he'd felt closest to her. She'd encouraged him, feeding his curiosity and nurturing his love for storytelling. In a way, it was her influence that had first led him to writing, a gift she'd passed on, even if she'd never quite known where it would take him.

Now, years later, the worlds in his mind had grown more real, more intense, and sometimes... darker. He couldn't help but feel that these imagined worlds were where he belonged, the only places that truly understood him. Real life, with all its noise and obligations, felt distant and blurred, like a television talk show on mute.

Standing here in the quiet of the cabin, that familiar ache settled over him, the sense that, no matter where he went, he'd always feel slightly out of place. It was a loneliness he couldn't shake, one that had driven him to create stories in his head—to build worlds where he felt he belonged.

He smiled softly, thinking of his mother. She'd have loved a place like this, so quiet and unassuming, a blank canvas waiting to be filled. Maybe, in some way, he'd come here for both of them, seeking a connection to that lost sense of closeness, hoping that in the solitude, he might find some piece of himself again.

Settling into the silence, he let his thoughts drift back to the life he'd left behind. To the constant demand for words, to the feeling of being drained dry, of giving pieces of himself away with every story. He'd written fifty stories—some bestsellers, some obscure—and each had taken a part of him, leaving behind a faint sense of loss. This cabin was meant to be a retreat, a place to recover what he'd lost. He wanted the silence to settle into his bones, to fill the hollow spaces left by too many words.

But even as he tried to relax, he found himself mentally narrating again, the words slipping in unbidden.

"He stares out the window, watching the trees bend under the weight of snow..."

He caught himself, shook his head. Old habits. Just his mind working in overdrive. But the words felt...separate from him. Detached. He brushed the thought away, determined not to let the quiet get to him.

Finally, he wandered through the rest of the cabin. The bedroom was small, just a bed and a dresser, the sheets still crisp from being freshly laundered. The bathroom was even smaller, with an old-fashioned sink and a narrow shower. Each room was barren, stripped of personality, but that was part of the appeal. A blank canvas. A place where he could carve out a space for his mind to roam, free of distraction.

But as he moved from room to room, he felt the quiet closing in again, heavy and watchful. His footsteps barely made a sound on the worn wooden floor, and he realized with a jolt that he was holding his breath.

"He moves to the window," his mind narrated softly. *"He glances outside..."*

He froze, caught off guard by his own inner voice slipping into real-time, narrating his movements just before he made them. His pulse quickened, the silence settling into something almost tangible, a presence he couldn't see but could feel, pressing against him, waiting. He turned slowly, feeling the weight of his own gaze on his shoulders as he glanced back into the main room, half-expecting to see someone there.

But it was empty, only Sativa stretched out on the floor, her eyes half-lidded, watching him with the patient, unblinking stare of a creature who saw more than he ever would.

Damien shook his head, forcing himself to let go of the tension coiling in his chest. It was just him. Just an empty cabin. He'd been alone before, many times, in places just as remote as this. But this quiet—it was different. Less a peaceful silence, more...deliberate.

Trying to shake off the feeling, he lit a fire in the stone fireplace, watching the flames catch and rise. The crackling warmth filled the room, casting shadows that danced on the walls, giving the cabin a life of its own. Sativa curled up nearby, her breathing slow and even, a small comfort in the growing darkness.

He settled onto the couch, trying to relax, to let the silence become part of him. The fire popped and crackled, filling the room with a warmth that felt almost protective. And yet, as he closed his eyes, he found his mind drifting, the words slipping in once again, soft and insistent.

"He feels the darkness pressing in, as though it's alive..."

Damien opened his eyes, startled. The firelight flickered, casting strange shadows on the walls. And there, in the corner of the room, Sativa sat with her back arched, staring intently into the darkness, her tail flicking back and forth like a pendulum.

For a moment, he didn't dare move, his heart thudding in his chest. The silence pressed down, thick and smothering, as if something waited just beyond the edge of the firelight, lurking in the dark. And in that moment, he wondered if he was truly alone.

Chapter Two: The Echoes of Isolation

The morning light seeped through the single window, filling the cabin with a muted grayness that felt like an extension of the snow-covered mountains outside. Damien squinted, slowly coming to as he became aware of Sativa perched at his feet, her gaze fixed on him with a look of stern disapproval.

"Morning, judgey," he mumbled, rubbing his eyes. "You're up early. Don't tell me you're hungry already?"

Sativa tilted her head, ears flicking in what he imagined was her version of a scoff, then turned with deliberate precision, tail lifted high as she trotted toward the kitchen. He watched her, feeling a tug of familiarity that settled his nerves—a sense of routine, even here. He stretched and rose, his joints protesting, then followed her, stifling a yawn.

In the kitchen, Sativa had taken her place by the empty bowl, sitting with a regal stillness as she waited for him to fill it. Damien chuckled, shaking his head.

"I see how it is," he said, crouching to pour her food. "Here I am, thinking I'm getting away from it all, and you're over here enforcing my schedule like clockwork."

Sativa didn't even glance up. Her gaze was laser-focused on the bowl as it filled, ears twitching as if to punctuate his words with a silent but emphatic *Yes, I am.*

Damien straightened, feeling a flicker of warmth pierce the quiet that had settled around him since he'd arrived. Having Sativa here grounded him, brought a touch of life to the stillness of the cabin. He took a deep breath, trying to let that comfort settle over him, to shake the strange feeling that had lingered since last night—the feeling that he wasn't quite alone.

As he moved about, organizing his scattered notes and making himself a cup of coffee, he became aware of the voice in his mind—the voice that had begun narrating his every movement the moment he'd stepped foot in the cabin. Today, though, it was quieter, softer, almost dormant. A good sign, he thought. Maybe yesterday had just been the result of his mind unwinding, his brain finally letting go after months of churning out stories.

But even so, he found himself lingering by the window, staring out over the snow-covered ground. The silence felt more pronounced here, each sound swallowed up as soon as it left, as if the world was holding its breath.

"Well, looks like it's just you and me, kid," he said, glancing down at Sativa. She had finished her breakfast and was now sitting by the door, staring intently at the narrow sliver of daylight shining through the crack. "Planning an escape? Or just sizing up the snow?"

Sativa turned to him, her eyes narrowing. She let out a small chirp, her way of acknowledging his presence, before resuming her vigil at the door. He shook his head, watching her, imagining her as a sentry, the last guard against whatever mysteries lay hidden in the snow.

"Guess you'd better let me know if anything's out there," he said, half-joking, but there was a weight to his words that surprised him. As if the idea of something out there wasn't as far-fetched as he wanted to believe.

He made his way to his writing desk, settling into the chair with a sigh. Today, he'd hoped to start something new—a fresh story, a new world to dive into. But as he stared at the blank page, his mind refused to focus. Instead, his thoughts drifted to the silence, how it filled the cabin, pressing in on all sides, thick and impenetrable. It was comforting, yes, but also... different. Restless, like it held secrets it wasn't ready to share.

"You think I'm just losing it, don't you?" he said, glancing over at Sativa, who had wandered back to the window, eyes glued to something he couldn't see.

Sativa ignored him, her focus unwavering. He squinted, following her gaze, but saw nothing beyond the vast expanse of white and shadow, the trees standing silent and still like frozen sentinels. A sudden chill ran down his spine, and he cleared his throat, rubbing his hands together as if to chase away the sensation.

"All right, nothing out there," he said, more to himself than to her. "Guess it's just the quiet getting to me."

Sativa let out a small, throaty chirp in response, as if humoring him. She sauntered over to him, leapt onto the table, and circled his laptop once before sitting, her gaze now fixed on him.

Damien sighed, shaking his head. "Don't judge me. Not everyone has it as easy as you, you know."

He reached out, scratching the top of her head, feeling the faint rumble of her purr beneath his fingertips. It was a small sound, but in the quiet of the cabin, it felt magnified, a reminder that he wasn't completely alone. He took a deep breath, letting the sound ground him.

But even as he stroked her fur, the voice in his head began again, a faint whisper, soft but insistent.

"He reaches out, hand trembling slightly, as though afraid of what he'll find..."

He froze, his hand suspended in midair, the narration slipping ahead of him, guiding his thoughts before he could shape them. The words lingered, haunting him, before fading back into silence, leaving him with a sense of disquiet he couldn't shake.

"All right, that's enough," he muttered, as though speaking directly to the voice itself. "I came here to get away from all that."

He pulled his hand back and stood up, trying to shake off the tension settling in his shoulders. His gaze drifted once more to the window, and this time, a faint flash of movement caught his eye—a blur against the white. He tensed, squinting, but the snow held nothing unusual, only the stillness of the trees and the thick blanket that covered the ground.

"You saw that, right?" he said, glancing at Sativa, who had now positioned herself back at the door, her eyes narrowed.

She turned to look at him, her tail flicking once in response, as if answering a question he hadn't quite asked. He let out a shaky laugh, pushing away the creeping dread.

"You're supposed to be my guard, remember?" he said, trying to keep his tone light. "No freaking me out with the whole 'staring into the void' thing."

Sativa gave him a look, one he swore held a spark of amusement, before turning back to the door, her tail swishing slowly as she resumed her vigil. He watched her, a small comfort returning as he allowed himself to sink into the rhythm of her movements, the graceful way she moved through the room, her calm presence a balm to the unsettled feeling he couldn't explain.

Still, as he moved through the cabin, his mind wandered back to the strange sense of familiarity that had settled over him since he'd arrived. He felt as though he knew this place, though he was certain he'd never been here before. It was as if the cabin held pieces of memories he'd long forgotten, fragments of dreams he'd had and lost somewhere in the depths of his mind.

He sat down once more, pen in hand, determined to push through the lingering fog and write. But the page remained stubbornly blank, and his thoughts drifted again, each one slipping from his grasp as soon as he reached for it.

Finally, he sighed, tossing the pen aside. "Some retreat this is," he muttered, glancing over at Sativa. "I came here to escape, and I'm just... spinning my wheels."

Sativa, sprawled on the windowsill, gave him a sidelong glance, her eyes half-closed, as though indulging him with her attention.

"Thanks for the sympathy," he muttered, chuckling softly. "Maybe I should've just brought my books and left the writing at home."

A flicker of movement caught his eye again, and he turned, feeling his heart skip a beat as he saw something—or thought he did—just beyond the trees. But when he looked again, the world outside was as empty as it had ever been, the snow untouched.

"Nothing out there," he murmured, more to himself than to her. "Just my mind playing tricks."

But as he turned away, he caught a faint shadow in the corner of his eye—a suggestion of movement just on the edge of his vision. And though he knew he was alone, he couldn't shake the feeling that someone, or something, was watching him, hidden in the silence that pressed in on all sides.

He glanced back at Sativa, who was watching him with an intensity that felt almost human, her green eyes narrowing slightly as though she sensed his thoughts.

"Guess it's just you and me, kid," he said softly, his voice barely more than a whisper. "Hope you're ready to hold down the fort."

Sativa blinked, and for a moment, he could almost believe she understood.

Chapter Three: First Signs of Dread

The silence had a way of thickening here, Damien thought, especially in the dim light of morning when shadows stretched across the floor, pooling in the corners like dark secrets. He sipped his coffee, watching the steam curl and twist above the mug, trying to shake the residual tension that had settled into his shoulders.

Sativa had perched herself on the arm of the couch, her eyes fixed on him with an intensity that felt almost confrontational.

"Do I get any privacy around here?" he asked, setting down the mug. She blinked, slow and deliberate, then glanced away, her tail flicking once as if in mild irritation.

"All right, I get it," he said, scratching the back of his neck. "I'm acting like a lunatic, talking to you like you're going to answer me."

Sativa ignored him, instead focusing on something in the corner of the room, her ears flattening slightly, her gaze unblinking. Damien followed her line of sight but saw nothing—a few scattered belongings, a worn chair, the faded shadows cast by the morning light. Yet Sativa continued to stare, and a faint chill crept up his spine.

"What's so interesting over there?" he muttered, crossing the room to adjust his things. "Is it a bug?"

He moved to the table, stacking his notebooks and rearranging his papers, trying to ground himself in the familiar.

But even as he worked, he could feel the silence pressing in, a thick, almost physical presence that seemed to hover just beyond his reach. His mind, that ever-present narrator, started again, slipping into real-time as he moved.

"He shuffles the pages, searching for something to anchor him, though he doesn't know what..."

Damien froze, his fingers hovering over the stack of paper. He hadn't thought those words; they'd arrived on their own, unbidden, as though someone else had slipped them into his mind. For a moment, he could almost feel it—a presence, distant but deliberate, guiding his thoughts, weaving them like threads into a narrative he couldn't control.

He shook his head, forcing himself to breathe. Just his mind playing tricks again. He'd come here to clear his head, after all, and maybe this was all just... noise, the residue of stories left unwritten.

But the voice persisted, slipping in as he resumed his work, each phrase feeling like an echo of something he couldn't quite hear.

"Every step he takes feels premeditated, as though he's following a path carved long before he arrived..."

He shut his eyes, willing the words to stop, to dissolve into the silence. And when he opened them, the room was still, the only movement the faint, steady rise and fall of Sativa's breathing.

"All right, Crowe," he muttered, rubbing his temples. "Get it together."

But just as he started to turn away, his gaze fell on something he hadn't noticed before—a small object sitting in the far corner of the room, half-hidden in shadow. It looked like a tiny bucket, no bigger than his fist, the dull gleam of its metal catching the light. He took a step closer, squinting, his curiosity prickling with a sense of unease.

"What's that, Sativa?" he asked, glancing at her. She was still watching him, her green eyes narrowed, as though she too sensed something was wrong.

The bucket was tarnished, the metal rough and pitted, with what looked like small objects inside. He knelt, hesitantly reaching out, fingers brushing the cold metal as he lifted it into the light. Tiny, jagged shapes glinted from within—teeth. Dozens of them, small and sharp, gathered in a perfect, miniature replica of the bucket of teeth he'd described in *The Witch of Blackwood Hollow*.

He swallowed, feeling his pulse quicken. It couldn't be. That detail... it was from a story, a piece of fiction, something he'd conjured from his own mind. And yet here it was, real and solid in his hands, as if it had slipped out of his pages and into his life.

He stared at it, half-expecting it to dissolve in his grasp, but the weight was undeniable, the jagged edges of the teeth biting into his fingers as he held it.

"Sativa," he whispered, glancing up at her. She was watching him intently, her eyes wide, ears pinned back as if sensing his unease. "Did you...? Have you seen this?"

She didn't respond, of course, but her tail lashed from side to side, a warning, her gaze darting between him and the bucket in his hand.

Damien set the bucket down carefully, his fingers trembling. His mind buzzed with questions he couldn't answer, with a fear that pulsed just below the surface, insistent and unyielding. It was just a coincidence, he told himself, forcing the words through clenched teeth. A strange, inexplicable coincidence, nothing more.

He backed away from the bucket, his eyes fixed on it as though it might suddenly leap from the floor. Sativa padded over to him, pressing her head against his leg, her presence grounding him, steadying his nerves. He reached down, his hand finding the familiar warmth of her fur, her purr vibrating softly under his fingers.

"You're seeing this too, right?" he whispered, glancing down at her. She looked up at him, her expression inscrutable, then nudged his hand as if to reassure him. For a moment, he felt a flicker of relief, a touch of normalcy in her presence.

But even as he petted her, the voice crept back in, a faint whisper in his mind, as though slipping through a crack in his defenses.

"He holds the cat close, a small comfort against the dread settling in his bones..."

Damien froze, his hand stilling as the words lingered, pressing into his thoughts like an unwelcome guest. He didn't want to believe them, didn't want to give them form or substance. But they felt... alive, more than just echoes in his mind. He swallowed, his gaze drifting back to the bucket of teeth, as if it held answers he didn't want to uncover.

In a sudden rush, he grabbed the bucket and shoved it into a drawer, slamming it shut with a force that rattled the cabin's quiet. Sativa leapt back, her tail puffing up in alarm, and he winced, feeling a pang of guilt.

"Sorry," he muttered, his voice a hushed apology. "I just... didn't want it out there. Didn't want to look at it."

THE STORIED MIND

Sativa seemed to consider him for a moment, then, with a flick of her tail, she jumped onto the couch, curling up as if nothing had happened. Damien watched her, a strange mixture of comfort and dread settling over him as he sank into a chair across the room.

The cabin seemed darker now, the shadows stretching across the floor as though reaching for him. He rubbed his temples, trying to shake the feeling, but the voice in his head had settled, a low hum that refused to be silenced.

He stared at his empty notebook, trying to focus, to write, to do something that might ground him in the real world. But the words slipped from his mind, each thought dissolving before he could capture it, replaced by the steady, unyielding pulse of that other voice.

"He sits alone, surrounded by silence, as the cabin settles around him, each creak a whisper of something just beyond..."

He shut the notebook, his heart pounding. This was supposed to be his retreat, his escape, the place where he could lose himself in his work. But now, it felt more like a prison, the walls closing in, the silence pressing down, heavier and darker than he could bear.

"Sativa?" he called, his voice small, barely more than a whisper. She lifted her head, her green eyes shining in the dim light, watching him with a patience he didn't deserve.

He forced a smile, hoping it might somehow break the tension. "I don't suppose you have any advice for me, do you?"

Sativa blinked slowly, a silent response, and then, as if answering his question in the only way she knew how, she stretched out on the couch, her tail curling around her like a shield. He watched her, feeling a pang of envy for her calm, her unshakeable sense of self.

The cabin settled around him, the silence stretching out like a shadow, enveloping him in a quiet that felt far from empty. Damien took a deep breath, leaning back in his chair, trying to shake the feeling that something—or someone—was watching him from the shadows.

He closed his eyes, letting the darkness settle over him, hoping that the quiet would ease the tension in his mind. But even as he drifted into a restless stillness, the voice lingered, a faint whisper on the edge of his thoughts, pulling him deeper into a world he wasn't sure he wanted to enter.

Chapter Four: Shadows in the Corners

THE FIRE HAD BURNED down to embers, casting a low, flickering light that barely reached the far corners of the room. Outside, snow fell in a steady curtain, muffling all sound beyond the cabin walls. Damien sat alone at the table, his notebook open in front of him, pages blank and waiting, as he searched for words that refused to come.

Sativa lay stretched out on the couch, eyes half-lidded, her breathing slow and steady. She seemed at ease, though her ears twitched every so often, picking up sounds he couldn't hear. Damien watched her, taking small comfort in her calm, letting the sound of her breathing fill the silence that had settled thick and heavy around him.

"What do you think, kid?" he asked, his voice low, a murmur meant more for himself than for her. "Maybe I'm out of ideas. Or maybe... maybe I'm just too tired to find them."

Sativa blinked slowly, unperturbed, then rolled onto her side, stretching her paws out in front of her. Damien smiled, feeling a flicker of warmth at her indifference. To her, this was just another quiet night. But to him, the silence felt almost oppressive, as if something hidden in the shadows was pressing in, waiting for him to notice.

"He stares at the notebook, lost in thought," the voice whispered, slipping in before he could silence it.

"His fingers hover over the page, though he doesn't know what he's reaching for..."

Damien's hand froze above the notebook, his pulse quickening. The words felt intrusive, invasive, as though they had been spoken aloud, slipping into his mind without permission. It wasn't his own voice—not the one he knew, not the one he trusted. This voice was... colder. Detached. Like a narrator who watched from a distance, unaffected and indifferent.

"Enough man," he muttered, closing the notebook with a snap, the sound echoing in the quiet.

Sativa lifted her head, eyes narrowing, watching him with a curiosity that felt almost too keen. She tilted her head, ears twitching, as though sensing something just beyond his reach.

"Sorry, girl," he said, forcing a chuckle that sounded hollow even to his own ears. "Didn't mean to wake you. Just... arguing with myself again."

She stared at him for a moment longer, then settled back down, her tail curling around her like a shield. He envied her calm, her unshakable confidence in her own reality. For her, the world was simple—eat, sleep, watch, repeat. She was unbothered by shadows, unburdened by the weight of silence. She was... safe.

But even as he thought this, he noticed her gaze shift, her eyes following something unseen along the wall, her ears flattening as her body tensed. Damien's breath caught, his pulse pounding in his ears as he turned to look. The firelight flickered, casting strange shadows that seemed to stretch and shift along the walls, but nothing moved. The room was empty, save for the worn furniture and the faded glow of the embers.

"What're you looking at girl?" he asked, his voice barely more than a whisper. Sativa's gaze remained fixed on the wall, her eyes narrowing, a low rumble rising in her throat. Damien felt a chill creep up his spine, settling in his bones, as he watched her.

The silence pressed down, heavier than before, as though the room itself was holding its breath, waiting. His own voice whispered in his mind, low and insistent.

"He turns slowly, afraid of what he'll see..."

Damien clenched his fists, fighting the urge to follow the words, to give in to the voice that seemed to know his every thought. But the compulsion was strong, almost physical, pulling him toward the shadows, urging him to look.

"Bullshit," he muttered, shaking his head. "This is just… bullshit."

But even as he tried to convince himself, he could feel the voice settling deeper, a presence he couldn't shake, weaving itself into his thoughts, blurring the line between what was real and what wasn't. He looked down at Sativa, hoping for some comfort, some sign that she hadn't noticed anything amiss.

But she was watching the corner of the room with an intensity that bordered on fear, her ears pinned back, her body coiled and ready, as if preparing to flee.

The fire crackled, a sharp, sudden sound that echoed in the silence, and Damien turned instinctively, his eyes catching a flicker of movement—something in the corner, just on the edge of his vision. He froze, his breath hitching, heart pounding as he stared.

At first, he thought it was just a shadow, a trick of the light. But as his eyes adjusted, he saw it—something folded into the corner, limbs twisted and bent at unnatural angles, as though it had been shoved into a space far too small for its body. Its eyes gleamed in the low light, dull and unfocused, yet somehow aware, watching him with a patient, unblinking gaze.

Damien's stomach twisted, his mouth going dry as he struggled to process what he was seeing. It looked... human, but wrong, each limb contorted in ways that defied anatomy, joints bending where no joints should be, skin stretched taut over bone. It didn't move, didn't breathe—just stared, its head tilted at an angle that felt both curious and mocking, as though it knew something he didn't.

A strangled sound escaped his throat, part gasp, part strangled whisper. He wanted to look away, to close his eyes and pretend it wasn't there, but the voice in his mind held him fast, whispering with a quiet, merciless certainty.

"He sees it now, the shape in the shadows, watching him with a hunger that goes beyond sight..."

Sativa let out a low hiss, her fur bristling as she backed away, her gaze locked on the twisted figure in the corner. Damien felt his own body tense, every instinct screaming at him to run, to leave, to escape whatever nightmare had crawled into his life. But his legs felt heavy, rooted to the floor, as though the very cabin had claimed him, trapping him in its grasp.

He swallowed, forcing himself to breathe, to move, to break the hold the figure had over him. Slowly, he backed away, his eyes never leaving the corner, even as he stumbled, nearly tripping over the edge of the table.

"Sativa," he whispered, his voice tight with fear. "Come on... let's... let's go..."

She didn't need further urging. In a single, fluid motion, she darted across the room, her sleek body a blur as she leapt into his arms, pressing close, her body trembling against his chest. He clutched her, his fingers buried in her fur, grounding himself in her warmth, her presence, as he backed toward the door.

But the figure didn't move. It remained still, twisted and folded into the shadows, watching him with a patience that felt almost... expectant. As though it knew he'd be back.

With a shaking hand, he reached for the door, fingers fumbling with the latch, his heart pounding as he yanked it open, the cold air rushing in, sharp and biting. He didn't dare look back as he stepped out into the snow, his breath coming in short, shallow gasps, Sativa pressed against his chest, her purr now a low, steady rumble that seemed to vibrate through his entire body.

For a long moment, he stood there, his body tense, eyes scanning the empty expanse of snow, half-expecting to see something lurking in the shadows of the trees. But there was nothing. Only the silence, thick and suffocating, pressing in from all sides.

He let out a shaky breath, glancing down at Sativa. She looked up at him, her eyes wide and unblinking, as though sharing in his fear, her tail flicking nervously against his arm.

"What the hell was that?" he whispered, his voice barely audible over the sound of his own heartbeat.

She didn't answer, of course. But in that moment, he felt a strange sense of understanding pass between them, a silent acknowledgment that whatever he'd seen... it was real.

They stood there together, two fragile lives huddled against the vastness of the night, as the cabin loomed behind them, its dark windows watching, waiting, as though it held secrets that neither of them were ready to face.

Finally, he turned away, clutching Sativa to his chest, and headed back inside, bracing himself against the cold, the silence, and the growing dread that had settled in his bones. But as he crossed the threshold, he couldn't shake the feeling that he was leaving something behind—a piece of himself, something vital and real, that would never quite find its way back.

And as he closed the door, he felt the silence settle around him once more, pressing down with a weight that was far from empty.

Chapter Five: The Descent into Madness

THE SILENCE OF THE cabin had changed. It was heavier now, as if it had taken on a shape of its own, filling the space with a presence that watched, waited, even breathed in rhythm with him. Damien lay in bed, staring up at the ceiling, his mind tangled in the remnants of uneasy dreams. Sativa curled beside him, her body pressed close, her quiet purring the only sound in the room.

The clock on the wall ticked softly, each second stretching longer than the last, as though time itself had slowed to a crawl. The fire had died down, leaving only a faint glow of embers that barely reached the edges of the room. Shadows pooled along the walls, slipping into the corners, shifting with a subtlety that made them seem almost alive.

He closed his eyes, trying to settle his racing thoughts, willing sleep to come, to offer him a brief escape from the mounting tension that had wrapped around him since he'd arrived. But just as he began to drift, he felt Sativa shift beside him, her body tensing, her purring fading into silence.

He opened his eyes, glancing down at her, and found her staring intently across the room, her eyes wide, unblinking. He swallowed, his pulse quickening as he followed her gaze. There, near the floor by the door, something dark and twisted jutted from the shadows—a bent limb, thin and pale, folded at an unnatural angle.

He blinked, his vision blurred with sleep, his mind struggling to make sense of what he was seeing. It was the figure—the same one he'd seen in the corner, twisted and bent, somehow fitting itself into an impossibly small space, as though it were squeezing into the dark just to watch him. He could barely make out its form, only a few details—the stretch of pale skin, the angle of a misshapen limb, and, just visible through the dim light, a single eye staring at him, lifeless and glassy, yet filled with a strange, patient awareness.

His breath caught, his chest tightening as he tried to focus, to understand if he was truly seeing it. But as he blinked, clearing the fog of sleep from his vision, the figure was gone, leaving only the empty shadow where it had been.

He lay there, frozen, his heart pounding as he strained to see any sign of movement, any trace of what he'd glimpsed. But there was nothing—only the shadows, thick and heavy, wrapping around the room in silence.

Sativa let out a low, anxious trill, pressing herself against him, her body trembling. He stroked her fur, trying to calm her, but his own nerves felt frayed, his mind spinning as he tried to reconcile what he'd seen. It had to be a trick of the light, he told himself. An illusion brought on by exhaustion, by the eerie stillness that seemed to have taken hold of the cabin.

But even as he lay there, reassuring himself, he couldn't shake the feeling that he wasn't alone. That whatever he'd seen was still there, hidden just beyond his sight, folded into the shadows, waiting for him to let his guard down.

The inner voice slipped in, soft and insistent, weaving through his thoughts.

"He closes his eyes, knowing that when he opens them, the shadows will be watching..."

Damien shut his eyes, willing the voice to stop, to dissolve into the silence, to let him sleep. But the image lingered, burned into his mind, filling his thoughts with a dread he couldn't shake. And as he drifted back into restless sleep, he felt the weight of its gaze pressing in, a silent reminder that he was not alone.

Chapter Six: The Madness Deepens

THE CABIN FELT COLDER tonight. Damien sat alone by the dwindling fire, watching the last embers fade into a dull glow, their warmth barely reaching across the room. Sativa lay curled up on the couch, her sleek black form a small comfort in the surrounding darkness. Outside, the snow fell steadily, a curtain of white that hid the world from view, leaving only the cabin and the silent, endless woods.

He glanced at his notebook on the table, the page still blank despite his best efforts to write. The words wouldn't come. His mind felt clogged, weighed down by a presence he couldn't see but could feel, thick as smoke in his lungs. And then there was the voice. That voice in his head, narrating his every movement, his every thought. He'd tried to ignore it, to drown it out with silence, but it had become relentless, seeping into every corner of his mind.

"He sits alone in the dark, his gaze drifting to the window, where shadows move just beyond the glass..."

Damien's head snapped up, his heart pounding as he stared at the window, half-expecting to see something there. But there was only darkness, the faint reflection of his own weary face in the glass. He took a deep breath, trying to steady himself. It was just his mind, he told himself. Just exhaustion, isolation.

He'd wanted solitude, hadn't he? He'd come here to escape, to find himself in the quiet. But the quiet had a way of filling up the space, of pressing down until it felt like it was inside him, choking him.

Sativa stirred on the couch, her ears twitching as she lifted her head, her gaze fixed on something he couldn't see. Her eyes were wide, alert, and Damien felt a chill run down his spine. He glanced around the room, his pulse quickening as he tried to see what had caught her attention. But there was nothing—only shadows.

"What do you see, girl?" he whispered, his voice barely audible. Sativa didn't respond, her gaze still fixed on the same spot, her body tense as if ready to spring.

"He turns to the window, drawn by a presence he can't explain..."

The words slipped into his mind, cold and insistent. He felt his legs move of their own accord, carrying him toward the window despite the fear clawing at his throat. He placed his hand on the glass, feeling the chill seep into his skin as he peered out into the snow-covered woods.

At first, he saw nothing. Only the trees, tall and dark against the white landscape, their branches heavy with snow. But as he squinted, his breath fogging up the glass, he caught a flicker of movement at the edge of the tree line. Something small, barely more than a shadow, but it was there, standing perfectly still in the snow.

His stomach twisted as he strained to see, his eyes adjusting to the dim light. And then he saw her—a little girl, her form thin and twisted, her face pale and gaunt, with a wild, feral grin stretched across her blood-smeared face. She was watching him, her gaze fixed on him with an intensity that felt almost... familiar.

She lifted a small, bloodied hand, and he realized, with a sickening jolt, that she was holding a severed arm, her fingers wrapped around it like a macabre plaything. She raised it in the air, waving at him as though greeting an old friend, her grin widening to show teeth that were sharp and jagged, yellowed with decay.

Damien stumbled back, his heart pounding as he tried to tear his gaze away. But he couldn't. He was rooted to the spot, his hand pressed against the glass, his breath coming in shallow gasps as the girl continued to wave, her eyes locked onto his with a knowing glint.

"She waves at him, a silent greeting, her grin wide and wicked, a memory come to life..."

"No, uh uh," he whispered, shaking his head. "That's... this isn't real..."

But the girl remained, her form solid and unmistakable, her eyes gleaming with a dark intelligence that made his skin crawl. She was from his book, from *Cold Cuts*—a twisted figment of his imagination, a character he'd created in a moment of horror. She wasn't supposed to be here. She couldn't be.

"Go away," he muttered, his voice a desperate plea. But she didn't move, didn't blink. She simply stood there, waving with that severed arm, her blood-soaked grin never faltering.

Finally, Damien tore himself away from the window, stumbling back as he tried to shake the image from his mind. His heart raced, his skin cold and clammy as he backed into the wall, pressing himself against it as if it could shield him from the horrors outside.

Sativa let out a low, distressed yowl, darting off the couch and circling his legs, her tail puffed up, her eyes wide with fear. He knelt down, his hands trembling as he reached for her, burying his fingers in her fur, grounding himself in the warmth of her presence.

"It's not real, girl," he whispered, more to himself than to her. "It's just… my mind. Just something wrong with me. Something's wrong with me."

But even as he spoke, he could feel the girl's gaze lingering, her presence pressing against the cabin like a weight. She was out there, waiting for him, watching, as though she'd come to life just for him, a creation turned nightmare.

For hours, he sat there, clutching Sativa to his chest, his gaze darting back to the window, half-expecting to see her there again. But the snow remained undisturbed, the woods empty and silent, as if she had never been there at all.

As the night wore on, Damien finally drifted into a fitful sleep, plagued by dreams of twisted figures and whispering shadows. He saw the little girl again, her grin wide and gleeful as she waved at him, her eyes bright with a hunger that went beyond the physical. She chased him through the snow, her laughter echoing in his ears, a sound that was both childlike and inhuman.

He awoke with a start, his heart pounding, sweat drenching his skin. The fire had gone out, leaving the room cloaked in darkness, and he could hear his own breath, shallow and ragged, filling the silence.

But then, another sound—faint, almost imperceptible, but there. A soft tapping, like fingers drumming against wood, coming from the far side of the room.

THE STORIED MIND

He froze, his eyes wide as he strained to see through the darkness, his mind racing as he tried to make sense of the sound. But there was only silence, thick and heavy, pressing in from all sides.

"He listens, the silence alive with secrets, the darkness filled with things he cannot see..."

The voice slipped into his mind, cold and calm, as if it belonged to someone else entirely. He tried to shake it off, to drown it out with his own thoughts, but it was relentless, a steady, insistent presence that seemed to know him better than he knew himself.

And then he saw it—a flicker of movement, just on the edge of his vision. He turned slowly, his heart pounding, his body tense with fear. There, in the corner of the room, he saw the figure, twisted and contorted, its limbs folded into impossible angles as it crouched in the shadows.

Its face was barely formed, features smeared and uneven, eyes in the wrong places, but it watched him with an intensity that left him breathless, as though it knew his every thought, his every fear.

Damien shut his eyes, willing it to disappear, to dissolve back into the darkness. When he opened them, the figure was gone, leaving only the shadows in its place.

Morning came, but the fear remained. Damien barely left his bed, clutching Sativa close, his mind racing as he tried to make sense of the nightmares, the visions, the voice in his head. He felt like he was coming undone, unraveling from the inside out, his thoughts slipping through his fingers like sand.

He didn't dare look out the window, didn't dare face the tree line where the girl had stood, her severed arm waving in greeting.

He couldn't shake the feeling that she was still there, hidden in the shadows, waiting for him to let his guard down.

"He clings to his sanity, but it slips away, each moment dragging him closer to the edge…"

The voice whispered in his mind, calm and steady, as though it had always been there, guiding him, pushing him. He tried to silence it, to block it out, but it was relentless, weaving itself into his thoughts, blurring the line between his own mind and something darker.

Finally, he forced himself to move, to break free from the paralysis that had gripped him. He stumbled to the window, peering out into the snow, half-expecting to see the girl, the twisted figure, the horrors he had created come to life.

But the woods were empty, the snow pristine, untouched. He let out a shaky breath, relief flooding through him, though it was tinged with a lingering sense of dread. He turned away, his thoughts a tangle of fear and confusion, his grip on reality slipping further with each passing moment.

Sativa brushed against his leg, her presence a small comfort, grounding him in a reality he could barely hold onto. He scooped her up, holding her close, her purr vibrating softly against his chest.

"We'll get through this," he whispered, more to himself than to her. "We'll… be fine."

But even as he spoke, he knew the words were hollow, a desperate attempt to hold onto something real in a world that had become a nightmare.

And in the silence that followed, the voice slipped back in, soft yet insistent, threading itself through his thoughts like a shadow.

"Damien Crowe... a name that was never his."

The words sank into him, unsettling and unfamiliar, as if he were hearing a truth he'd long tried to bury. He'd lived under that name, worn it like a second skin, given it to his stories as if it were his own. But now, standing there in the dark, holding Sativa close, he felt a creeping dread—the feeling that "Damien Crowe" was just a mask he'd worn, something fragile and borrowed.

And as the voice continued to whisper, he felt a tremor of fear deep within him, a growing certainty that he wasn't entirely sure who he really was.

Chapter Seven: Shadows and Hauntings

The room was dark, thick with the kind of silence that presses down from all sides, muffling every sound. Damien awoke suddenly, his mind still tangled in remnants of half-formed dreams. He squinted in the faint glow from the nightstand, eyes catching the harsh red numbers of the clock. *4:44 a.m.*

A shiver crawled up his spine as he stared at the numbers, an inexplicable sense of dread settling over him. But it wasn't the time that held his attention—it was the sound. A low, continuous rumble, so soft he almost missed it. He turned his head, blinking as his eyes adjusted, and saw Sativa at the edge of the bed, her body arched, fur standing on end, as she stared intently at the bedroom door. Her lips were pulled back in a snarl, a low, throaty growl spilling from her throat.

"What is it, girl?" he whispered, his own voice trembling as he glanced at the door, half expecting to see something lurking in the shadows. But the doorway was empty, only darkness spilling in from the hallway beyond.

And then a faint creaking sound, like someone shifting weight just outside the bedroom. The hair on the back of his neck stood on end, a chill running down his spine as he stared at the door, his heart pounding. The creaking was followed by a waft of something hot and foul, a thick, nauseating stench that clung to the air, making his stomach churn.

He held his breath, straining to hear, to see, hoping he was just imagining things. But then another creak sounded, closer this time, as though something—or someone—was standing just outside his line of sight, hovering by the door. Sativa let out a sharp, angry hiss, her eyes narrowed, her gaze unblinking.

Damien's mouth went dry, dread settling over him like a heavy blanket. "Who's there?" he managed, his voice little more than a whisper.

A wet, guttural sound filled the room—a horrible, sickening throat-clear, as if something were gargling from deep within. The sound was thick and sticky, the kind that sent a jolt of nausea twisting through his stomach. He felt frozen, trapped, unable to look away from the darkness just beyond the door.

Then, just as suddenly as it had come, the sound faded, leaving only silence in its wake. The stench lingered, though, clinging to the air, thick and oppressive. Sativa's growl softened, but she remained tense, her gaze still fixed on the doorway, her ears flat against her head.

Damien's thoughts spun, his mind racing as he tried to shake the image, the sound, from his head. And then, a chilling realization washed over him. He'd written this scene before—the creaking, the stench, the terrible throat-clearing sound—all of it had come straight from the pages of *The Witch of Blackwood Hollow*, a story he'd written years ago. But how could that be? How could it be here, haunting him, like a memory he couldn't escape?

A deep unease settled over him, a disorientation he couldn't shake. He glanced at the clock again, the numbers glaring at him as if mocking him. *4:44 a.m.* He turned away, trying to push the thoughts from his mind, but his gaze fell on his phone on the nightstand. He picked it up, blinking at the date. *September 12th.*

His birthday.

The knowledge filled him with a strange, hollow sadness, a deep ache that seemed to eat away any feeling. He'd never celebrated his birthday, it was always just another day to him. But now, he tried to forget the day even existed. 2 years ago, while waiting for his yearly happy birthday call from his father, he instead received news he hadn't been prepared for.

It was the day his father had died. He'd been waiting by the phone, expecting the familiar sound of his father's voice, his clumsy attempts at a birthday greeting. But instead, there had been silence, a hollow ache that lingered long after he'd hung up.

He shook his head, trying to push the memory aside, to bury the pain that had resurfaced, raw and jagged. Sativa had settled back down, her gaze still wary, her body tense as she lay curled up by his side.

As the first faint light of dawn crept through the window, Damien took a deep breath, willing himself to move, to break free from the hold of the memory. But his inner voice slipped back in, soft and insistent, whispering in his mind.

"He looks outside, drawn to the shadowed woods, to the presence waiting just beyond his sight…"

He clenched his jaw, pushing the voice away, determined not to look, not to give in. But the urge gnawed at him, the voice slipping back with every moment of silence, urging him to see what lay beyond the window.

The day passed in a fog, each hour stretching endlessly as the voice continued, prodding, urging, filling his mind with images of shadows, of figures waiting just outside his line of sight. He tried to focus, to ignore the voice, but it was relentless, unyielding.

By evening, he was exhausted, every nerve frayed, his mind teetering on the edge of something he couldn't name. And then, just as he was beginning to think he could ignore it, he heard it—a faint tapping, rhythmic and steady, coming from somewhere nearby.

He froze, his heart pounding as he listened, straining to pinpoint the sound. It seemed to come from outside, but he couldn't be certain. The tapping continued, persistent and unyielding, filling the silence until it was all he could hear.

The inner voice returned, weaving through his thoughts, coaxing, urging him to look, to see what waited beyond the glass.

He crossed the room, his movements slow, deliberate, as he approached the window. He placed his hand on the glass, feeling the chill seep into his skin as he peered out into the snow.

At first, he saw nothing—only the trees, tall and dark against the fading light. But then, a figure emerged from the shadows, standing at the edge of the tree line.

Damien's breath hitched as he recognized the figure, his heart lurching painfully in his chest. It was his father, standing there in the snow, his face pale, eyes wide and unblinking, fixed on Damien with a look of quiet expectation.

"Hey, son," the figure called, his voice soft, familiar. "Come here. Oh yeah, happy birthday. Come on out, let's watch some movies. Got some Kung Fu Theater, and Godzilla is coming on in a minute. Come here..."

THE STORIED MIND

The words struck him like a blow, each one filling him with a hollow ache, a sorrow that went beyond words. He felt his throat tighten, his vision blurring as he stared at the figure, his father's face etched in the same lines he remembered, the same expression he'd missed all these years.

He tore his gaze away, the pain too real, too raw to bear. He stumbled back, pressing his fists against his temples, willing the image to disappear, to dissolve back into the shadows where it belonged.

As he staggered back to his bed, his mind a haze of grief and confusion, he lay down, closing his eyes, hoping to escape the torment that filled his thoughts. But the voice slipped in again, quiet and insistent, whispering in his mind.

"And as he rolls over, the sight of horror strikes him..."

He opened his eyes, a sinking dread settling over him as he turned, half-expecting nothing more than shadows.

But there, inches from his face, was a contorted figure, folded into the space beside him, its skin wet and glistening, oozing with a thick, viscous fluid. Its face was barely formed, features smudged and dripping, an eye rolling slowly down its cheek as it stared at him, its expression twisted into a grotesque imitation of a smile. *"Happy Birthday"* it gurgled.

A strangled cry escaped his throat, his body paralyzed with fear as he took in the sight, the horror of it pressing down on him like a physical weight. He scrambled back, heart pounding, his breath coming in shallow gasps as he stumbled to his feet, bolting from the room.

He barely registered the cold as he burst through the front door, his bare feet sinking into the snow as he stumbled forward, the icy air biting into his skin. He ran to his car, throwing open the door, Sativa at his heels, her growls mingling with his own ragged breaths as he fumbled with the keys, jamming them into the ignition.

He turned the key, desperate, but the engine only sputtered, refusing to start. His hands shook, his heart pounding as he tried again, the car silent, unyielding.

A low growl from Sativa made him turn, his gaze following hers to the edge of the woods. There, emerging from the shadows, was the entire cannibal family from *Cold Cuts*, their faces twisted, their bodies smeared with blood, each one holding a different severed body part. Their eyes gleamed with hunger, their lips curled into grins that were all teeth and malice.

Damien's heart raced as he grabbed Sativa, pulling her close, his mind a whirlwind of fear and confusion. He stumbled back into the house, slamming the door behind him, his breaths coming in ragged gasps. He held Sativa tightly, feeling her body tense in his arms, her low growl a steady vibration against his chest. The cabin loomed around him, its shadows deeper, heavier, as though they had thickened in the darkness, pressing down from all sides.

His mind spun, struggling to make sense of what he'd just seen. *The family from Cold Cuts*, the very characters he'd created in a fit of horror and despair, now standing in the snow, their bloodstained faces grinning, their eyes fixed on him with an intensity that felt too real, too visceral.

The voice slipped in again, calm and steady, weaving through his thoughts.

"He stumbles back, clutching the cat as the walls close in, the darkness tightening around him like a shroud..."

THE STORIED MIND

He shook his head, pressing his hands to his temples, willing the voice to stop, to dissolve into silence. But it was relentless, slipping into every corner of his mind, filling his thoughts with images of shadows, of figures lurking just beyond his line of sight, waiting for him to let his guard down.

Sativa squirmed in his arms, her claws digging into his shoulder as she twisted, her gaze fixed on something he couldn't see. He followed her line of sight, his pulse racing as he scanned the room, half-expecting to see the twisted figure lurking in the shadows, its melting skin dripping onto the floor.

But there was nothing—only silence, thick and oppressive, pressing down like a weight he couldn't shake.

He stumbled toward the window, his breath fogging up the glass as he peered outside. The tree line was empty, the snow undisturbed, as if the horrors he'd seen had vanished into thin air, leaving only the lingering dread in his chest.

But the voice continued, soft and insistent, whispering in his mind.

"He knows the truth now, knows that the horrors he created have come to life, he knows they're realer than he has ever been..."

"Shut the fuck up," he whispered, squeezing his head, his voice barely more than a breath. "This isn't real. Somethings just wrong with my mind. They've been telling me this for years. It's just a condition. I'm fine, I'll be fine..."

But even as he spoke, he felt the truth settle over him like a shadow, a cold, unyielding presence that refused to be ignored. The line between his stories and reality had blurred, slipping away until he could no longer tell where one ended and the other began.

The voice slipped in again, a final, chilling whisper that echoed in his mind, filling him with a dread he couldn't escape.

"He has become like his stories, and they have become like him. He's no realer than they are. And if they aren't real, then neither is he..."

And as he stood there, clutching Sativa in the silence, he felt the weight of his own creations pressing in from all sides, filling the cabin, the shadows thickening, deepening, as though waiting for him to let them in. In the distance he could just barely make out the faint sounds of *The Phantom Finders* crew going on another ghost hunting mission. He knew none of this could be real. But what that meant about him, filled him with even more dread.

Chapter Eight: The Pull of Madness

DAMIEN'S HANDS TREMBLED as he bolted the door, the weight of everything he'd seen pressing down on him like a heavy fog. He could still feel the cold from outside seeping into his bones, and the unsettling images from his nightmares—the cannibal family, his father at the tree line, the contorted figure—clung to him like shadows that wouldn't fade. His head buzzed with a silent urgency, a ringing that settled behind his eyes as he backed away from the door and into the depths of the cabin.

Sativa darted past him, her tail fluffed up, her movements sharp and erratic. She paced the edges of the room, stopping at darkened corners, her gaze fixed as though she could see things he couldn't. She would stand there, tense, then dart away, her low growls the only sound breaking the silence.

"Settle down, girl," he muttered, but his voice wavered, uncertain. He caught sight of himself in the reflection of a glass picture frame on the wall and flinched at the pale, wide-eyed figure staring back at him. He averted his gaze quickly, avoiding his own reflection, as if afraid of what he might see there.

He stumbles, turning away from the window, avoiding the glass that betrays him...

The voice slipped in, calm and quiet, narrating his every movement with a precision that unnerved him. It had become relentless, as if it had sunk into his thoughts, weaving itself into the very fabric of his mind. He felt like a puppet, each step dictated by the words that spilled into his thoughts before he even knew what he was going to do.

Damien shook his head, trying to block it out, to take back control of his own actions. "Get out of my head," he whispered, clenching his fists, his fingers digging into his palms. "You're not real... none of this is real."

But even as he spoke, he could feel his grip on reality slipping, as though something else—some force, some unseen presence—had woven itself into the walls of the cabin, into the very air he breathed. He stumbled over to a drawer in the living room, yanking it open in search of anything that might anchor him—a flashlight, a notebook, anything.

Instead, he froze. Nestled in the drawer was a worn paperback, its cover scuffed and faded, but unmistakable. He knew that book—*Endless Quest: Choose Your Own Doom Chronicles*. But it wasn't his book. This was the actual choose-your-own-doom book he'd written about years ago, a fictional artifact he'd crafted as part of a horror series. He reached out, his hand trembling as he picked it up, staring at the familiar, battered cover.

"This... isn't possible," he whispered, his voice barely audible.

He flipped it open, his fingers grazing the pages, feeling the weight of his own creation in his hands, a book that shouldn't exist in the real world. The words stared back at him, each line familiar, each choice leading the reader deeper into doom. He could feel his pulse racing, a sick thrill mixed with dread, as

THE STORIED MIND

though he were holding something forbidden, something dangerous.

With a sudden burst of panic, he slammed the book shut, clutching it in his hands as he stumbled to the door. "You're not real!" he shouted, hurling the book outside. It landed in the snow with a soft thud, its pages fluttering as it settled, leaving an eerie, unnatural silence in its wake.

He slammed the door shut, his breathing ragged as he backed away. "This isn't happening," he muttered, his voice shaking. "It's... it's all in my head."

He throws the book outside, desperate to banish the shadows of his own making...

Damien squeezed his eyes shut, willing the voice to stop, but it only grew stronger, the words echoing in his mind with each movement, each thought, describing his own horror as though he were nothing more than a character in a twisted story.

A low, guttural sound broke through the silence, a faint, rhythmic chanting that made his skin crawl. The words were muffled, unintelligible, but unmistakable. He recognized the cadence, the sinister lilt—it was the chant he'd written in *Satanic Panic*, a book about a group of kids who stumbled upon a cult ritual. He shook his head, trying to dispel the sound, to convince himself it was just his imagination.

But the chanting continued, growing louder, filling the room with a presence that felt heavy, oppressive. He covered his ears, backing away from the sound, his eyes darting around the room as if he might see the cultists materialize before him, drawn to his fear.

"Stop it," he whispered, his voice a desperate plea. "Just... stop."

But the voice continued, relentless, narrating his fear, his horror, describing his desperation as he backed away, as if feeding off his own thoughts, twisting them into a nightmare he couldn't escape.

He stumbles, retreating from the shadows that surround him, the voice growing louder, drowning out his own thoughts...

With a shudder, he turned toward the kitchen, hoping to escape the chanting, to find some corner of the cabin untouched by the horrors he'd created. But as he opened a drawer by the counter, his breath caught in his throat, his heart pounding as he saw it.

The figure was there again, folded into the small, cramped space of the drawer, its limbs bent at impossible angles, its skin slick and oily, glistening in the dim light. Its face was barely recognizable, features twisted and smudged, but its eyes—its eyes stared up at him, dark and unblinking, as though daring him to acknowledge its presence.

Sativa hissed, her fur bristling as she backed away from the drawer, her gaze fixed on the figure. Damien let out a choked laugh, a sound that bordered on hysteria, his voice trembling as he pointed at the figure.

"See? You're real!" he shouted, his tone veering between triumph and terror. "You're not in my head—you're here, you're real! I'm fine, and you're not!"

The figure didn't move, didn't blink, its eyes locked onto his with an intensity that made his skin crawl. He stumbled back, the laughter dying in his throat as he slammed the drawer shut, his breathing ragged as he tried to steady himself.

Sativa pressed against his leg, her growl a low, steady vibration, as though grounding him in the reality he could no

THE STORIED MIND

longer trust. He reached down, his hand shaking as he stroked her fur, feeling the warmth of her presence, the steady rhythm of her purring.

But the voice continued, whispering in his mind, its words cold and unfeeling, narrating his every thought, his every fear.

He clings to the cat, his only anchor in a world that has turned against him, his creations come to life, his nightmares real...

Damien sank to the floor, his back against the wall, pulling Sativa into his lap as he buried his face in her fur, clinging to her as though she were the only thing tethering him to reality. The chanting had faded, but the silence that followed was thick, suffocating, pressing down on him like a weight he couldn't shake.

He closed his eyes, willing the voice to stop, to leave him in peace, but it was relentless, slipping back in with each moment of quiet, filling his mind with images of shadows, of twisted figures lurking just beyond his line of sight, waiting for him to let his guard down.

And in that silence, he felt a cold, creeping realization settle over him—a truth he had tried to ignore, to deny. His creations had come to life, seeping from the pages of his own stories, filling the cabin with a darkness he couldn't escape. They weren't just in his mind; they were here, real, as real as the air he breathed, the shadows that surrounded him.

And he was their prisoner.

The voice slipped in again, soft and insistent, weaving through his thoughts with a chilling certainty.

"There is no escape. He has become his stories, and they have become him. The shadows are real, and they are here to stay."

He opened his eyes, his gaze drifting to the window, the darkness beyond seeming to pulse with a life of its own, as though watching him, waiting for him to surrender.

And in that moment, he knew that he would never truly be alone again.

Chapter Nine: The Descent into Isolation

Damien sat hunched over his notebook, his pen trembling in his hand as he tried to write. His thoughts felt scattered, slipping away with each attempt to form a coherent sentence, his mind tangled in a web of dread. Each word he put down felt hollow, meaningless, as if the act of writing itself had turned against him.

"Write your way out," he whispered to himself, clutching the pen with a desperation that bordered on madness. *"Take back control, you wrote them in, write the fuckers out..."*

But as he wrote, the inner monologue grew louder, more insistent, slipping in between his thoughts with a mocking tone that twisted his every word.

"He writes in vain, clinging to the hope that his words can save him, yet each line only pulls him deeper into his own nightmare..."

He clenched his jaw, forcing himself to ignore the voice, to drown it out with the scratch of his pen on paper. But the words felt thin, lacking the weight they once had, as though they no longer belonged to him. His own thoughts felt foreign, distant, slipping away as quickly as he tried to hold onto them.

Just then, a faint sound broke through his focus—a soft, rhythmic banging, like someone pounding on wood. He paused, his heart quickening as he listened, the sound growing louder, more insistent, until it echoed through the cabin like a drumbeat.

He turned, his gaze darting to the windows, where shadows shifted, dark and formless, pressing against the glass. The banging intensified, a chorus of pounding fists and guttural growls that sent a shiver down his spine. Sativa hissed, her fur bristling as she backed away from the window, her gaze fixed on the darkness outside.

Damien's heart pounded as he strained to see through the dim light, to make out the shapes that loomed beyond the cabin walls. And then he saw them—figures, twisted and unnatural, their bodies hunched, skin stretched tight over sharp, bony limbs. Their eyes gleamed in the darkness, reflecting the faint light with a hunger that sent a wave of nausea through him.

The banging grew louder, more frenzied, as if the creatures were desperate to get inside, their hands clawing at the door, rattling the windows. He could hear snarling, guttural voices, the sound of teeth gnashing, of claws scraping against wood. And then, amid the chaos, he heard something else—a scream, high-pitched and desperate, a voice he recognized.

"Dana, run!" the voice yelled, panicked, filled with terror. "They're coming—get away!"

Damien's blood ran cold. *Dana.* The name struck him like a blow, and his mind reeled with a sickening realization. It was a name from his own book, *Skin of the Moon.* He could hear the characters he'd created, the teens he'd put through a world of horror and nightmares, crying out as the skinwalkers tore through them, ripping flesh from bone with a hunger that was all too real. He could hear Dana Pleading with him, begging him to let her in, asking him why he would create her and her friends

THE STORIED MIND

only to have them be ripped apart every time someone reads them, screaming at him about how cruel he is to do this to them, to make this their existence.

He stumbled back, his chest tight with fear as he tried to block out the sound, but the screams continued, echoing through the cabin, filling his mind with images of blood and carnage. He could hear the tearing of flesh, the crunch of bones, the wet, sickening sound of bodies being torn apart, each sound sinking into him like a hook, pulling him deeper into his own nightmare. "No," he whispered, shaking his head, his voice a desperate plea. "This... this isn't real. It's just... it's just a book..."

But even as he spoke, he felt the truth pressing in, heavy and undeniable. His creations had come to life, slipping from the pages of his own stories, filling the cabin with horrors he could no longer escape.

The inner monologue slipped back in, cold and mocking, feeding off his fear.

"He realizes now that his stories have betrayed him, that the horrors he created have come to life, dragging him into a world he cannot escape..."

"No!" he shouted, his voice breaking as he stumbled away from the desk, his gaze darting around the room, searching for some way out. But there was nowhere to run, nowhere to hide from the creatures that pressed against the walls, snarling, growling, their claws scraping against the wood, desperate to get in.

Sativa hissed, darting to the far corner of the room, her eyes wide with terror as she watched the shadows shift and writhe, as though they were alive, pressing against the cabin from all sides. Damien could feel the walls closing in, the air thick with the scent of blood and sweat, the sounds of violence filling his mind with images he couldn't shake.

He backed away, his steps faltering as he turned toward his writing desk, hoping for some anchor, some reminder of reality. But there, folded into the small space between the chair and the wall, was the twisted figure, its limbs bent at impossible angles, its skin slick and oily, glistening in the faint light.

The figure stared at him, its eyes dark and unblinking, its face twisted into a grotesque smile that sent a shiver down his spine. It didn't move, didn't blink, but its presence filled the room, pressing down on him like a weight he couldn't escape.

Damien let out a choked laugh, a sound that bordered on hysteria, his gaze locked onto the figure as he spoke.

"See? You're real!" he shouted, his voice breaking. "You're not in my head—you're here, you're real! I'm fine, and you're not!"

But even as he spoke, the figure remained silent, its eyes locked onto his with a knowing intensity that made his skin crawl. It was as though it knew his fears, his doubts, as though it had been waiting for this moment, waiting for him to break.

The banging on the walls grew louder, more desperate, and he could hear the voices outside—Dana's screams, the shouts of other characters he'd written into existence, each voice a reminder of the horrors he'd created, the nightmare he'd unleashed.

His inner voice slipped in again, cold and relentless, narrating his every thought, his every fear.

"He stares into the darkness, realizing that his stories have become his prison, that there is no escape from the horrors he created..."

THE STORIED MIND

Damien sank to the floor, his hands pressed to his ears, his body shaking as he tried to block out the sounds, the screams, the snarls, the pounding on the walls. But it was relentless, the noise filling every corner of his mind, pressing down until he felt like he was drowning in his own nightmares.

Sativa crouched beside him, her eyes wide and fearful, her low growl a steady vibration against his side, as though grounding him in a reality he could barely cling to. He reached out, his fingers trembling as he stroked her fur, feeling the warmth of her presence, the steady rhythm of her purring.

But even as he held her, the voice continued, whispering in his mind, filling him with a dread he couldn't escape.

"He knows now that his creations are real, that they will never leave, never let him go. The shadows are here to stay. They are as real as him. If they're not real then neither is he..."

He closed his eyes, clinging to Sativa as though she were the only thing tethering him to reality, the only reminder of a world that made sense. But the shadows pressed in, the walls closing around him, as though the cabin itself had become part of the nightmare, a prison he could never escape.

And as he sat there, his mind unraveling, the voice continued, weaving through his thoughts, filling him with a final, chilling realization.

"He has become his stories, and they have become him. There is no escape. He doesn't exist"

He opened his eyes, his gaze drifting to the window, where the darkness loomed, thick and impenetrable, as though watching him, waiting for him to surrender.

Chapter Ten: Guilty Echoes

Damien drifted in a light, uneasy sleep, his mind hovering between dreams and the cold silence of the cabin. A faint tapping pulled him from the darkness, a soft but persistent sound, rhythmic and unrelenting. He stirred, rubbing his eyes, his mind sluggish, the weight of his earlier horrors pressing down on him.

The tapping continued, gentle yet insistent, drawing him toward the window. He blinked, adjusting his eyes to the dim light, and felt his heart skip, a dull ache throbbing in his chest. There, outside the window, stood a figure—a face he hadn't seen in years but knew as well as his own.

His childhood friend. His best friend, the one he'd thought lost to time and regret.

The boy smiled, his eyes soft and warm, just as Damien remembered them. He tapped lightly on the glass again, his hand resting against the windowpane, his expression calm, reassuring, as though he had simply come by to check in, to say hello.

Damien's breath caught in his throat, his chest tightening with a strange mix of longing and sorrow. He reached out, his fingertips brushing the cold glass, half afraid that the boy would vanish if he blinked.

"Is it... really you?" he whispered, his voice trembling.

The boy nodded, his smile widening, the same easy grin that had once been Damien's anchor in a world that often felt too big, too fast. The boy's lips moved, his words faint, barely audible through the barrier between them.

"It's okay, Damien. You're going to be okay."

Damien's heart twisted, a pang of guilt slicing through him. Memories flooded back, fragments of laughter, shared secrets, and a bond that had once been unbreakable. And yet, he had broken it, hadn't he? He'd left, selfishly, distancing himself in a moment when his friend might have needed him most. He'd always wondered if, somehow, his absence had been the cause, if his friend might still be here if he'd been there, if he hadn't...

But the boy's gaze held steady, his smile soft and understanding.

"It wasn't your fault," the boy whispered, his words gentle, like a balm on an old wound. "None of this is real, Damien. You're going to be okay."

Damien swallowed, his throat tight, a heaviness settling over him. The boy's words lingered, their weight pressing down, and for a fleeting moment, he felt as though everything might truly be okay. That this was nothing more than a dream, a figment of his own mind, that he could wake up and leave it all behind.

"I... I thought... maybe if I'd been there," he began, his voice barely more than a whisper. "I thought maybe you'd still be here..."

The boy's smile never wavered, his gaze warm, filled with a compassion that was almost otherworldly. "I know, Damien. But it wasn't your fault. I love you, and it's going to be okay. Just don't worry."

Damien felt his vision blur, his chest tightening as he reached out, pressing his hand against the glass, as though he might somehow bridge the gap between them, might somehow bring him back. But then, a sound broke the silence—a low, seething hiss, like something writhing in the shadows behind him.

He froze, the hair on the back of his neck prickling as the sound grew louder, filling the room with a visceral, angry pulse. He turned, his heart pounding, his pulse racing as he felt a hot breath brush against his skin, thick and humid, smelling of decay and rot.

There, just inches from his face, was the twisted figure, its limbs folded and bent in ways that defied reason, its skin slick and oozing, glistening in the faint light. Its face was a mess of features, eyes in the wrong places, its mouth stretched wide, a grotesque imitation of the boy's comforting smile.

It leaned closer, the smell of it suffocating, its body trembling with rage, as though barely containing the hatred that pulsed beneath its skin. Damien stumbled back, his heart pounding, but the figure followed, looming over him, filling his vision with its warped, nightmarish form.

And then it screamed, a sound that tore through him like a knife, its voice raw, primal, filled with an anger that seemed to reach into his very soul. The force of it sent him reeling, stumbling backward, his foot catching on the edge of the bed as he fell, the room spinning around him.

He landed hard, his breath knocked from his lungs, his gaze darting around the room, half-expecting to see the figure lunging toward him, ready to tear him apart.

But there was only silence, thick and oppressive, pressing down like a weight he couldn't shake. He scrambled to his feet, his gaze darting around the room, his heart racing as he searched for any sign of the twisted figure, of the boy who'd been at the window.

And then he saw it, nestled in the far corner of the room—a small shoebox, its lid slightly ajar, with a single, pale limb sticking out, twisted at an impossible angle. The sight of it sent a chill down his spine, a shiver that sank deep into his bones, as though the very air had turned cold, heavy with a presence he couldn't escape.

Sativa padded over, her eyes wide and wary, her gaze fixed on the shoebox as she let out a low, uncertain growl. Damien felt a tremor pass through him, his body shaking as he backed away, his thoughts a tangled mess of fear and confusion.

He looked back to the window, hoping for one last glimpse of his friend, for a reassurance that the nightmare was over, that the boy's words had been real, that he was, somehow, going to be okay.

But the window was empty, the faint light of dawn spilling through the glass, casting long shadows across the room, shadows that seemed to stretch and bend, taking on shapes that flickered at the edges of his vision.

Damien sank to the floor, his back pressed against the wall, clutching his knees to his chest as he stared at the shoebox, at the twisted limb that lay motionless, as though daring him to look closer, to acknowledge its presence.

And in the silence, the voice slipped back into his mind, quiet, insidious, filling his thoughts with a final, haunting whisper.

"He realizes now that his past is as real as his nightmares, that he will never truly be free of the shadows that haunt him, that

the boy at the window is nothing more than a memory, a ghost lingering in the dark..."

He closed his eyes, pulling Sativa close as he let the words wash over him, feeling the weight of his own guilt, his own regrets, pressing down like a shroud. The boy's words echoed in his mind, a faint, distant memory, slipping away with each passing moment, leaving only the silence, thick and unyielding.

And as he sat there, the cabin around him filled with shadows, he knew that he would never truly be alone again.

Chapter Eleven: The Breaking Point

THE CABIN WAS DARK, the only light a faint glow from the dying embers in the fireplace. Shadows clung to the walls, thickening in the corners, shifting like smoke. Damien sat alone on the floor, his back pressed against the cold wood, his knees drawn to his chest. He felt small, like a child, and the silence pressed down on him, heavy and unyielding.

His mind felt frayed, stretched to the breaking point. Memories he'd tried to bury clawed their way to the surface, each one bringing with it a wave of pain that felt like it might drown him. He could feel it—the raw ache in his chest, the tightening of his throat, the way his breath came in shallow, uneven gasps.

"Damien Crowe..." he whispered to himself, clinging to the name as though it were a lifeline. But the words felt hollow, distant, like an echo of someone else's voice. He wasn't even sure what it meant anymore, what he meant. Who was Damien Crowe? Was he even real? Or had he become just another character, a mask to hide behind?

The memories surged, unrelenting. His mother's face flashed in his mind, her soft smile, the way she'd always called him "B" with such tenderness. He'd been just a boy when she'd passed, left alone with a father who had struggled to cope, who had done his best but had never quite known how to be enough.

And then his father—gone, too, leaving Damien adrift, untethered, clinging to the only thing that had ever felt real: the stories he created. They'd become his world, his sanctuary, the only place where he felt he had any control. And yet, even that had slipped away, twisted and turned against him, leaving him lost in a nightmare of his own making.

And then there was his best friend. The memory of him surfaced, sharp and unforgiving. They'd been inseparable once, as close as brothers. But Damien had disappeared, retreated into himself, into his stories, leaving his friend behind when he might have needed him most. And when he'd returned, it had been too late. His friend was gone, and Damien had been left with a guilt that gnawed at him, a wound that had never healed. And then there were the others.... The others...

He pressed his hands to his temples, his fingers digging into his skin as he tried to block out the memories, to push them back into the darkness where they belonged. But they were relentless, clawing at him, filling his mind with images, with voices, with an ache that felt like it might tear him apart.

A soft, almost imperceptible sound broke through the silence—the faintest rustling, like fabric against wood, or the quiet shift of a shadow. Damien froze, his heart pounding, his breath caught in his throat as he looked up, his gaze darting around the room.

And then he saw her.

She was there, standing in the far corner, her figure barely visible in the dim light, a twisted silhouette against the wall. The witch from *The Witch of Blackwood Hollow*. Her body was a grotesque, contorted mass, her limbs bending at unnatural angles, her joints cracking and popping as she moved. Her face

THE STORIED MIND

was a horror of distorted features, her mouth stretched wide in a smile that was all wrong, her eyes dark and empty, fixed on him with a hunger that made his skin crawl. And there, just below her in the shoe box was the bent figure, cowering and looking up at her in fear, it's eyes dripping off of it's face.

The air grew thick, suffused with a nauseating stench of rot and decay, and Damien's stomach twisted as the smell enveloped him, filling his lungs, pressing down on him like a weight.

"No... no, this isn't real," he whispered, his voice trembling. "You're not real... you're just... you're just a story..."

But the witch only smiled, her face stretching, cracking, as though her skin were too tight, barely containing the horror beneath. She took a step closer, her movements slow and deliberate, each step accompanied by the sickening crack of bone, the wet, sticky sound of flesh twisting and tearing.

Damien scrambled back, pressing himself against the wall, his heart pounding as he watched her approach, his mind screaming at him to move, to run, but his body was frozen, paralyzed by the sheer, overwhelming presence of her.

The witch loomed over him, her twisted form filling his vision, her smell overwhelming, suffocating. She reached out, her fingers impossibly long and thin, curling around his shoulders, lifting him from the ground as though he weighed nothing. He dangled in her grasp, his body limp, his mind a haze of terror and disbelief.

The witch's face was inches from his own, her breath hot and rancid against his skin, her mouth stretched into a grin that felt like it would swallow him whole. Her gaze bored into him, dark and unblinking, as though she could see into the deepest corners of his mind, as though she knew every thought, every fear, every regret he'd ever buried.

"Please..." he whispered, his voice barely audible, a desperate plea. "Please... I didn't mean for any of this..."

But the witch's expression didn't change, her eyes cold and empty, devoid of any mercy. She tightened her grip, and Damien felt a sharp, searing pain shoot through his shoulders, the sickening crack of bone reverberating through his body.

And then he heard it—the wet, tearing sound, the sound he'd written into her character, a sound he thought existed only in fiction. It was a sound he knew too well, a sound he'd created, but now it was real, vibrating through him, filling him with a horror so deep it felt like it might consume him.

The world blurred, the shadows closing in, pressing down until he could no longer breathe, until he was nothing more than a fragment, a whisper, a shadow in the darkness. And then, silence.

Chapter Twelve: A Revelation

Damien drifted into awareness, his senses sluggish, as if struggling to surface from the depths of a dark, endless sea. The light was harsh, sterile—a flat, clinical brightness that made him squint. His body felt distant, foreign, as though it were something apart from him, and he realized he was lying on a narrow, uncomfortable bed, encased in cold sheets.

Muffled voices floated around him, distant at first, but gradually sharpening.

"...it's remarkable he even survived," one voice said, calm, detached, the tone of a doctor discussing a complex case. "If those rangers hadn't found him... well, I don't think we'd be talking about him in any state right now."

"Yes, sir," another voice responded, younger, more hesitant. "So, all of this... the breakdown, the alternate persona, the new pen name... it was all a coping mechanism?"

The first doctor sighed. "A coping mechanism, yes, but an extreme one. He's endured a lifetime of trauma and loss—most people wouldn't be able to withstand a fraction of it. The mind can only take so much before it finds a way to shield itself. In his case, it seems he crafted an entirely new identity to escape the pain—a character who could distance him from everything he wanted to forget."

There was a pause, and Damien's vision flickered, his gaze falling on a clipboard by the edge of the bed. He struggled to focus, his eyes catching on a name written in clear, clinical letters: *B. Humphrey*.

The words felt strange, almost foreign, and a chill crept down his spine as the sound of that name—*Mr. Humphrey*—rang in his ears, murmured by one of the doctors. *Humphrey.* Was that... him?

"Creating 'Damien Crowe' was a way for him to survive," the doctor continued, voice calm and professional. "It allowed him to block out who he was, to detach from his own pain. The stories he wrote became his reality, a place where he could hide from his grief, from everything that had made him feel different, isolated."

The younger doctor spoke softly. "So, you think he'll ever... come out of it?"

The doctor's voice took on a note of empathy. "I doubt he'll ever be the same. This sort of profound detachment, this blurring between fiction and reality—it's likely permanent. He's built his entire life on this narrative, one where his pain and losses don't exist. And now, well, he's unresponsive. Trapped, it seems, in the stories he created."

The words weighed heavily in the air, pressing down like the sterile light above. Damien's mind, numb and fogged, struggled to piece together fragments of memories—the faces of his parents, his friends, so many friends lost, so much loss, his childhood trauma, fragments of voices that felt at once familiar and foreign. They drifted past him, like scenes from a distant, half-remembered dream.

The doctors turned to leave, their voices growing softer. "In cases like these, reality has become too painful to face. He may be lost to his own creations. If he finds any peace, it may only be within his mind. It's tragic... but perhaps, given what he's endured, it's all he has left."

The footsteps faded, and silence settled over the room. Damien's eyes remained open, staring blankly at the ceiling. He couldn't move, couldn't speak, trapped within his own mind as the words echoed in his thoughts, cold and hollow.

"He'll never be the same. He'll never truly be okay."

His inner voice stirred, slow and uncertain, winding through his thoughts like a shadow slipping into place. It narrated each fragment of his existence with a quiet certainty.

He would go on, creating stories, living in them as if they were reality, so he would never have to face his own empty existence.

He felt a weight settle over him, the inevitability of it pressing down like a shadow. The memories faded, distant and blurred, as he slipped back into himself, into a world of his own creation, where reality no longer held sway.

The silence thickened, and just as the room settled into stillness, a faint sound broke the quiet—a soft creak, the slightest shift. The drawer by the bedside table slid open, just an inch, revealing a shadow within, the hint of something pale, a twisted limb, the edge of an eye staring back at him. Limbs twisted and folded in impossible angles.

The light faded, leaving only shadows, and in his mind, Damien felt the darkness close in, soft and familiar, swallowing him whole. And the stories began again.

Also by B. Humphrey

Retro Horrors: The Lost Decade
Cassette Ghosts
Summer of the Black Star
The Arcade Incident
Dead End Drive – In
The Polaroid Project
Endless Paths: The Choose-Your-Own Doom Chronicles
Neon Dreams
The Forgotten Carnival
Satanic Panic
Skin of the Moon

The Autumn Folklore Chronicles
The Forest Of Forgotten Names
The Witch Of Windspindle Hollow
The Burrowfolk Chronicles

The Phantom Finders Club

A Haunting On Maplewood Street
The Secrets Of Old Fort Tower
Ghosts OF The Infirmary

The Starling Sleuths
Detective Starling vol. 1
Detective Starling Vol. 2

Winter Horrors
Whispers of the Wendigo
Cold Cuts
The Dark Beneath

Standalone
The Witch of Blackwood Hollow
The Storied Mind

Milton Keynes UK
Ingram Content Group UK Ltd.
UKHW032222231124
451423UK00014B/1273